Die Riesenrübe

The Giant Turnip

Adapted by Henriette Barkow
Illustrated by Richard Johnson
German translation by Nick Barkow

Jahr für Jahr bauten die Kinder von
Fräulein Honeywoods Klasse im
Schulgarten Obst und Gemüse an.

Every year the children in Miss Honeywood's class grow
some fruit and vegetables in the school garden.

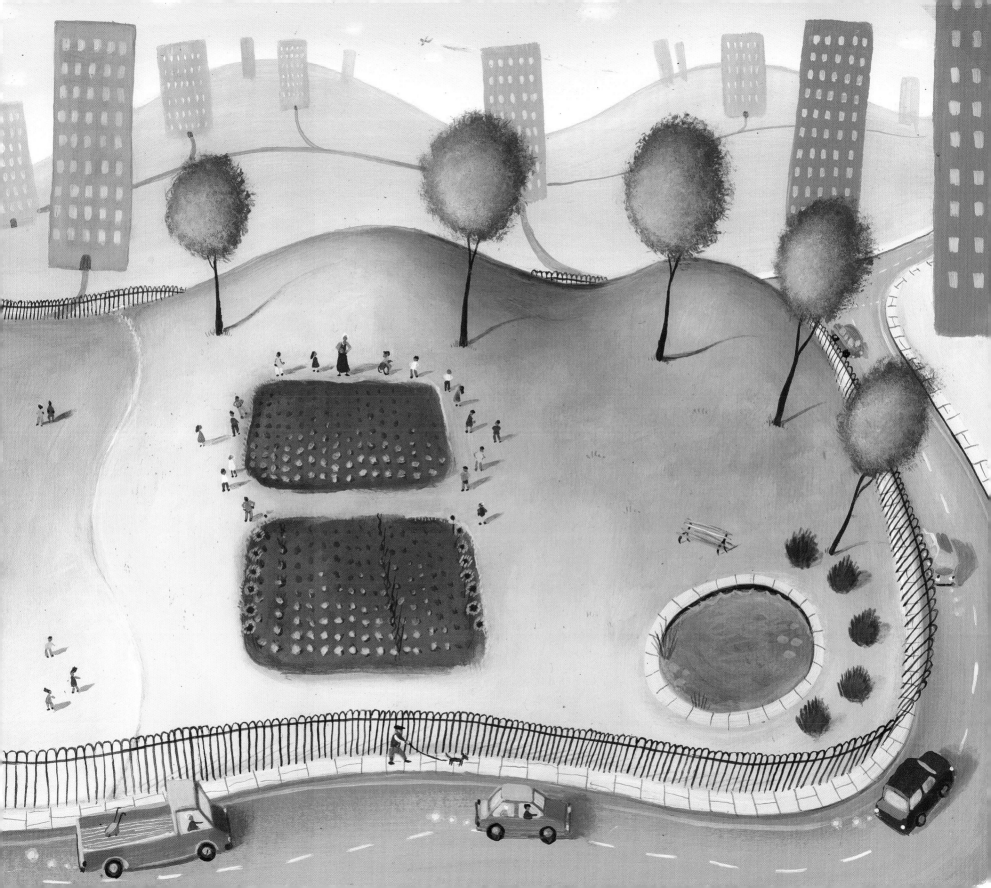

In diesem Jahr wollten sie anpflanzen

This year they decided to grow

Salat,

lettuces,

Radieschen,

radishes,

Mohrrüben,

carrots,

Tomaten,

tomatoes,

Sonnenblumen,

sunflowers,

Erbsen

peas

und Rüben.

and turnips.

Zu Frühlingsanfang bereiteten die Kinder erstmal
den Boden vor, sie gruben um und harkten ihn.

In early spring the children prepared the ground by digging and raking the soil.

Im Verlauf des Frühlings, als keine Frostgefahr
mehr bestand, pflanzten sie die Saat aus.

Later in the spring, when there was no danger of frost,
they planted the seeds.

Im Sommer gossen die Kinder die Pflanzen und düngten sie.
Und sie jäteten das Unkraut.

In the summer the children fed
and watered the plants.
And pulled out all the weeds.

Zurück aus den Sommerferien stellten die Kinder fest, dass Gemüse und Früchte gut geraten waren.

When the children came back, after their summer holiday, they found that all the fruit and vegetables had grown.

Dann sahen sie die Rübe. Sie trauten ihren
Augen nicht! Sie war grösser als eine
Giraffe und dicker als ein Elefant.

But when they saw the turnip, they could hardly
believe their eyes! It was taller than a giraffe,
and wider than an elephant.

Als sich Fräulein Honeywood von ihrem Schreck erholt hatte, fragte sie: "Wie kriegen wir diese Rübe raus?"

When Miss Honeywood had recovered from the shock, she asked, "How are we going to get the turnip out?"

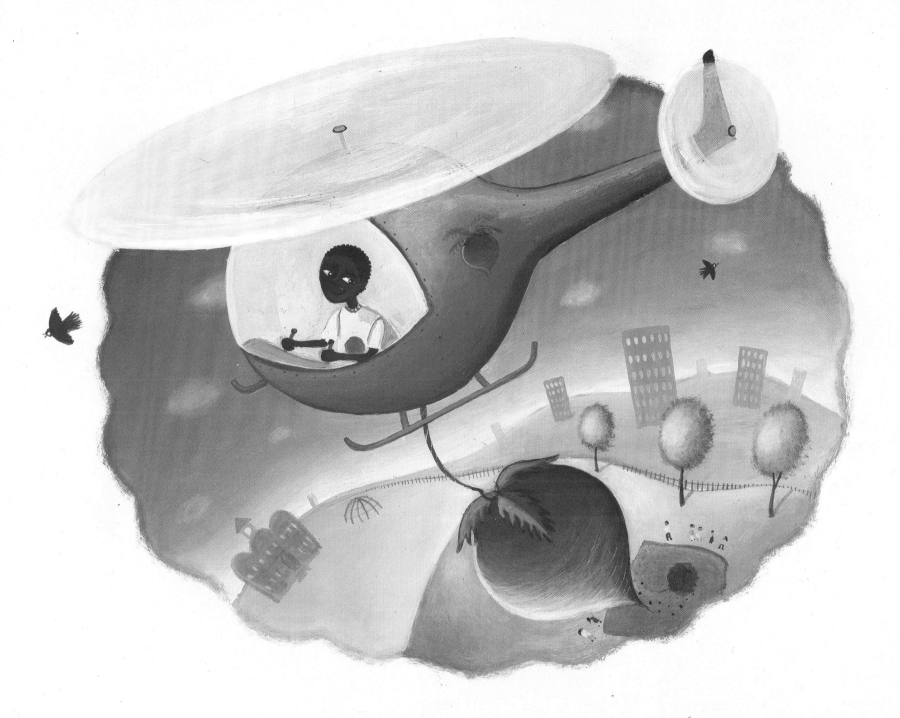

"Ich weiss," sagte Kieran, "wir holen einen Hubschrauber, der sie rauszieht."

"I know, we could get a helicopter to pull it out," said Kieran.

"Oder wir holen einen Kran, der sie raushebt," fand Tariq.

"Or we could get a crane to lift it," suggested Tariq.

"Oder einen Bulldozer, der sie ausgräbt," sagte Kate.

"Or a bulldozer to dig it up," said Kate.

"Wir könnten ein Seil dran festbinden und dann alle ziehen," schlug Samira vor.
"Das ist eine gute Idee," sagte Fräulein Honeywood.
"Lee und Michael, holt mal das lange Seil."

"We could tie a rope around it and all pull together," suggested Samira.
"That's a good idea," said Miss Honeywood. "Lee and Michael, go and get the long rope."

Die Kinder knüpften das Seil fest um die Riesenrübe. Gleich griffen sich die Jungen das Seil. Sie zogen und zerrten mit aller Kraft. Aber nichts geschah.

The children tied the rope around the enormous turnip. The boys grabbed the rope first. They pulled and pulled with all their strength but nothing happened.

"Wir sind stärker als die Jungs!"
riefen die Mädchen, und griffen
sich das Seil. Mit aller Kraft zogen
und zerrten sie. Aber die Rübe
rührte sich nicht vom Fleck.

"We're stronger than the boys!"
shouted the girls and they grabbed
the rope.
They pulled and pulled with all their
strength but still the turnip would
not move.

"Jetzt versuchen wir es mal gemeinsam," sagte Fräulein Honeywood. "Und wir zählen bis drei." "Eins, zwei, drei!" riefen die Kinder und zogen gemeinsam.

"Let's all try together," suggested Miss Honeywood. "On the count of three." "One, two, three!" shouted the children and they all pulled together.

Aber die Rübe rührte sich nicht.

But the turnip still would not move.

Da kam Larry an.
"Larry," rief Tariq, "wir brauchen
deine Hilfe!"
Larry lief ans Ende des Seils und
packte es an.
"Eins, zwei, drei!" riefen die
Kinder und zogen gemeinsam.

Just then Larry arrived.
"Larry!" shouted Tariq. "We need your help!"
Larry ran to the end of the line and grabbed
the rope.
"One, two, three!" shouted the children and
they all pulled together.

Die Rübe ruckelte ein wenig hin und her. Ganz allmählich bewegte sie sich. Gleich zogen sie noch einmal mit aller Kraft. Endlich rollte die Rübe aus dem Loch auf den Rasen.

The turnip wobbled this way and that, and then it slowly moved. They pulled even harder and at last the turnip rolled out of its hole and onto the grass. The class cheered and danced around with joy.

Am nächsten Tag hatten die Kinder der Klasse von Fräulein Honeywood das grösste Rüben Festmahl, das es je gegeben hat. Es blieb auch noch genügend übrig für alle Kinder der Schule.

The next day for lunch Miss Honeywood's class had the biggest turnip feast ever and there was enough left over for the whole school.

To Mum, Dad, Maggie & Ben
H.B.

For Sushila
R.J.

First published in 2001 by Mantra Lingua Ltd
Global House, 303 Ballards Lane
London N12 8NP
www.mantralingua.com

A CIP record for this book is available from the British Library